Healthy Eating

Sylvia Goulding

Rourke
Publishing LLC
Vero Beach, Florida 32964

PHOTOGRAPHIC CREDITS
Cover: **The Brown Reference Group plc:** Edward Allwright
Title page: **The Brown Reference Group plc:** Edward Allwright
The Brown Reference Group plc: Edward Allwright 3, 4, 11, 16, 18, 20, 22, 24; **Corbis:** 12, 26; **Hemera Photo Objects:** 6, 7, 8, 9, 11, 12, 13, 19, 23, 27; **RubberBall:** 10, 14, 28; **Simon Farnhell:** 4, 5, 8, 9, 11, 13, 17, 18, 19, 21, 23, 25.

FOR ROURKE PUBLISHING LLC
Editor: **Frank Sloan**
Production: **Craig Lopetz**

FOR THE BROWN REFERENCE GROUP PLC
Art Editor: **Norma Martin**
Picture Researcher: **Helen Simm**
Managing Editor: **Bridget Giles**
Design Manager: **Lynne Ross**
Children's Publisher: **Anne O'Daly**
Production Director: **Alastair Gourlay**
Editorial Director: **Lindsey Lowe**

With thanks to models **Natalie Allwright, India Celeste Aloysius, Molly and Nene Camara, Daniel Charles, Abbie Davies, Isabella Farnhell, Georgia Gallant, Connor Thorpe, and Joshua Tolley**

Important note: Healthy Kids *encourages readers to actively pursue good health for life. All information in* Healthy Kids *is for educational purposes only. For specific and personal medical advice, diagnoses, and treatment, and exercise and diet advice, consult your physician or school nurse.*

LIBRARY OF CONGRESS CATALOGING-IN-PUBLICATION DATA
Goulding, Sylvia.
  Healthy eating / Sylvia Goulding.
     p. cm. – (Healthy kids)
  Includes bibliographical references and index.
  ISBN 1-59515-204-0 (hardcover)
  1. Nutrition–Juvenile literature. 2. Health–Juvenile literature. 3. Children–Nutrition–Juvenile literature. I. Title. II. Series.

  RA784.G685 2004
  613.2–dc22

                                                    2004012277

Consultant: **Ramona Slick, R.N.,**
National Association of School Nurses (NASN)
A registered school nurse, Ramona looks after more than 600 students, from kindergarten to twelfth grade. Her students include many with special needs.

Some words are shown in bold, **like this**. You can find out what they mean by looking in the glossary on page 30.

Contents

Why do we...
Eat and drink?

▼ Sharing a meal with your friends is good fun. Why not organize a picnic?

We eat because we are hungry and we drink because we are thirsty. We need food and water to survive. Food makes us strong and fit. It gives us energy to play and work. It keeps us warm when it's cold. It refreshes us when it's hot. Food can stop you becoming ill, and it even makes you feel all-round happy.

Just amazing!

● **People eat the strangest things...**
● Some flowers are pretty and good to eat. Rose petals, lavender, and violets are all tasty if treated right.

● Dine on a dandelion! Next time, instead of blowing its seeds in the wind, cook and eat it, or brew it for tea.

What we eat...

...to fill us up *1*

...to gain strength *2*

...to share with friends *3*

Staple foods
You probably have these foods on most days: pasta, rice, potatoes, bread, breakfast cereals...

Fruit and vegetables
Apples, mangoes, pears, cherries; broccoli, yams, sweet potatoes. Can you think of any more?

Meat and poultry
Steaks, pork chops, lamb kabobs, chicken, turkey, and foods made from meat, like burgers and franks.

Dairy foods
Milk and foods made from milk, like butter, cream, cheese, and ice cream.

Seafood and fish
Food from rivers and the sea— shrimps, crab, crawfish, salmon, cod, and catfish.

We drink all these
Milk, soda, fruit juice, and water. Adults also drink coffee and tea.

Safety first!

● How would you like to have some seaweed for supper? Bite a bat? Or feast on a frog? Snack on a snail? Some people just love them...

!!!treat new foods with caution!!!
● Some foods can make you very ill. Always check with an adult before trying something you don't know.

Why is it good for me?
Starchy food

You may eat cereals for breakfast, bread for your sandwiches, and rice, pasta, or potatoes with your dinner. These **starchy** (STAR chee) foods are rich in **carbohydrates** (KAR bo HY drayts). They give you energy. They fill you up so you are no longer hungry. They are rich in **fiber** (FY bur). This is good for your stomach and your guts. It helps your body **digest** (DI jest) food so you stay healthy.

◄ *Eating carbohydrates gives you energy, and you will feel "full of beans."*

Or try this...

- Gorge on great grain feasts...
- couscous with carrot and raisins
- wholemeal rice with grilled peppers
- oatmeal with honey and yogurt

- Perfect pasta sauces...
- ham, broccoli, and mushrooms
- spinach and walnuts
- prawns in tomato sauce

Good or bad?

Grain facts

Check it out

Go shopping with your mom and compare different breads at the bakery counter. There are rye breads, bagels, and French loaves, for example.

Bad carbohydrates

All the goodness has been taken out of white bread, rice, or pasta. Eat wholemeal varieties instead. Cakes and other sugary foods also contain carbohydrates. They are not very healthy so eat them rarely.

eat wholemeal pasta

eat wholemeal bread

eat few cakes and cookies, sorry!

◀ Potatoes are good mashed, in salads, and baked in their skins.

● Try these super sandwich toppings...
● grilled baby tomatoes and cheese
● your favorite ham and bell peppers
● arugula leaves and grilled eggplant

Why are they good for me?
Fruits and vegetables

fruits and vegetables are crammed full of **vitamins** (VYT uh munz). Your body needs vitamins so you can grow and stay healthy. There are many different types—some are listed on page 9. Each one does a different job. Some make your gums, teeth, and hair strong. Some make your eyes powerful so you can see in color and find your way around in the dark. Others also make your blood clot when you have cut yourself. Vitamins even stop you catching colds. They do this by making your blood strong so it can fight germs and infections.

▲ *Laugh out loud— eating plenty of fresh vegetables and fruits can help you stay healthy.*

Just amazing!

● **Vitamins make you smart and pretty**
Eating fresh vegetables and fruits gives you a smooth skin, great fingernails, shiny, healthy hair, and an excellent memory!

Or try this...

● **Very nice vegetable treats...**
● noodle and beansprout stir-fry
● pumpkin seeds and carrot stick snacks
● pizza with a spinach, tomato, corn, and onion topping

Important vitamins

Vitamin A—good eyesight
apricots, mangoes, melons, lettuces, carrots, peppers, tomatoes, spinach

Vitamin B—energy
bananas, avocados, beans, broccoli, cauliflower

Vitamin C—fights diseases
oranges, grapefruit, potatoes, tomatoes

Vitamin K—clots blood
chicory, cauliflower, cabbages

▶ *There are so many fruits and vegetables to choose from. And they're all healthy!*

When you have a baked potato, eat the skin. It has even more vitamin C than an orange.

● **Fresh and fruity treats...**
● Enjoy wobbly gelatin with fresh strawberries.
● Pile blueberries and bananas into a pancake.
● Munch a mango sliced onto a waffle and topped with plain yogurt.

Why are they good for me?
Meat, fish, and dairy

Meat, fish, dairy foods, and eggs are all packed with **proteins** (PRO teenz). Proteins help you grow strong, tall, and happy. They make and repair your body **tissues** (TISH ooz) and **organs** (OR gunz). Without proteins your muscles cannot grow strong. All kinds of nuts and legumes like beans, lentils, and peas are also rich in proteins.

◄ *Like you, a pet dog gets its protein from meat. You, however, can also get protein from milk, eggs, and legumes.*

Safety first!

● To get enough protein...
● **Vegetarians** (VEJ uh ter ee unz) do not eat meat. Many eat no fish or seafood. Some don't eat anything to do with animals, like eggs or dairy foods. They are known as vegans (VEE gunz).
● If people cut out whole food groups— like meat, fish, or dairy foods—they need

Dairy foods

Strong and healthy

Milk and foods made from milk are called dairy foods. They include cream, yogurt, and cheese. Dairy foods have lots of vitamin D and **calcium** (KAL see um). They make your bones strong and stop them breaking. They make your teeth healthy. And they give you healthy hair and fingernails.

▼ *Make your burger healthier. Add lots of salad to a wholegrain bun. Leave out the mayo and the ketchup.*

▼ *If your fingernails often break and split, you probably need more calcium.*

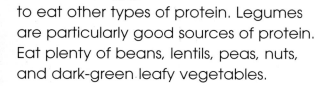

to eat other types of protein. Legumes are particularly good sources of protein. Eat plenty of beans, lentils, peas, nuts, and dark-green leafy vegetables.

Are they good for me?
Fats and sweets

We need to eat some fat, because it gives us energy. Fat also keeps us warm. There are two types of fat: good fats and bad fats. In most western countries we eat too much bad fat. We also eat too much sugar in candy, cakes, and cookies. This makes us **overweight** (o ver WAIT). It can also clog our blood vessels or cause **diabetes** (DYE uh beet ez) and **heart disease** (HART diz EEZ).

◀ *Are you tempted by candy floss? Have a piece of fruit instead!*

Or try this ...

- Eat less fat...
- Go easy on the mayo, ketchup, and other bottled sauces.
- Don't use too much butter or cream.

- Don't eat too much junk food— burgers, fish sticks, chicken nuggets.
- Cut off the fatty bits on meat, and eat "white" meat (chicken, turkey).

Which fat is good?

Bad guys

Eating too much animal fat is unhealthy. There are animal fats in meat and in foods that come from animals: milk, butter, cream, and cheese.

Good guys

Vegetable fats are very healthy. There are good fats in olives, peanuts, avocados, and brazil nuts. Oily fish also have good fats—try sardines, mackerel, tuna, and anchovies.

▲ *A melted cheese pizza topping tastes great, but don't eat it too often. It is full of fat and will make you put on weight.*

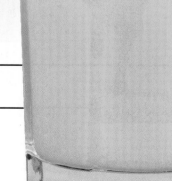

Or try this...

- When you feel like snacking on sweets...
- Munch dried apricots, pears, or raisins.
- Grab a handful of mixed unsalted nuts.
- Drink a glass of freshly squeezed orange juice.

How much of each food makes...
A balanced diet?

Your body needs a variety of different foods to be healthy. You should eat more of some foods than of others. The pyramid on the right shows you which foods you should eat the most. The pyramid is widest at the bottom because grains are the most important food. It is narrowest at the top because you should not eat too much fat.

▼ Eating some foods from every group makes you grow strong and healthy.

Quiz -?-?-?-?-?

1 A healthy lunch is...

A Eating nothing at all, so you can lose weight.

B Eating as many doughnuts and candy bars as possible.

C Eating a wholemeal sandwich with cheese and tomato, an apple, and a handful of nuts and raisins, plus drinking some fresh orange juice, for example.

Fats and sweets
Eat very little of these.

Dairy
Two servings a day:
• 1 cup of milk
• a small hand size
piece of cheese

Grains
Six servings a day:
• 1 slice of bread
• 6 tablespoons
of cooked pasta
or rice
• 1 small
pack of
cold
cereal

Meat and fish
Two servings a day:
• a small hand size piece
of lean meat, chicken, or fish

Fruits and vegetables
Five servings a day:
• 1 piece of fruit
• 1 small can of fruit
• 1 handful of dried fruit
• 1 glass of fruit or
vegetable juice
• 2 large spoonfuls
of cooked
vegetables
• 1 small plate
of fresh salad
vegetables

▲This pyramid shows how much you should eat from each
food group every day. Each example counts as one serving.

2 For a balanced diet it's best...
A to eat a mixture of foods from
different food groups
B to eat nothing on some days
C to eat only meat and eggs

3 Most children eat...
A just the right mixture
B too many sweets
C not enough fruit and vegetables

ANSWERS: 1C, 2A, 3B and C

Eating well

there's an easy-to-follow rule about eating healthy food. Try to eat "five a day." Not five cakes or candy bars, but five portions of vegetables or fruit! It's easy to do—a glass of fresh fruit juice counts as one portion, an apple or slice of melon counts as one, a serving of vegetables and potatoes with your main meal makes two servings. You only need one more: nibble on some dried apricots or peaches, and you're there.

◀ *There is some truth in the old saying "an apple a day keeps the doctor away." Eating a variety of fruits and vegetables helps you stay healthy.*

Or try this...

- To make sure you eat more fruit...
- Each time you go out to play, grab an apple or a banana to go.
- Snack attack? Chew on dried fruit.

- At a cook-out or BBQ, fill half your plate with meat, half with vegetables.
- At a self-serve buffet, pile vegetables and salads on your plate.

Eating by color

A rainbow of foods

Bright colors in vegetables and fruits are a good sign. They show that the foods are packed with healthy vitamins and minerals. Choose a variety of different colors.

green (good for bones and teeth): green apple, green grapes, kiwi, honeydew melon, broccoli, avocado, okra, and spinach

red (good for the heart): red apple, red grape, cherry, strawberry, red pepper, radish, and tomato

white (good for the heart): banana, date, cauliflower, onion, and mushroom

yellow/orange (makes you active and fresh): orange, mango, apricot, pineapple, carrot, pumpkin, and squash

blue/purple (good for your memory): blueberry, blackberry, black grape, plum, eggplant, and red cabbage

Just amazing!

● Not all bananas are yellow. There are more than 100 types. Some have red skin!
● Are all raspberries red? Most are red, but some are black, white, or yellow.

● Eating a variety of different colored fruits and vegetables every day protects you from some cancers, heart disease, stroke, brittle bones, and other diseases.

eating...
Too much

Your body turns the food you eat into energy. Food energy is measured as **calories** (KAL uh reez). Even if you lie still in bed all day, you need to eat 1,200 calories every day. Men need to eat more than women. Active people need to eat more than inactive ones. But most of us eat many more calories than we need!

◄ *Eat too many chocolate bars and you will end up putting on weight.*

Or try this...

● **Are you overweight?**
● See the school nurse. She will measure your BMI (body mass index). This tells you if your weight is fine, or if you are overweight or **obese** (o BEES).

● **If you are overweight or obese...**
● Avoid junk food and sugary drinks.
● Turn off the television set, video games, and the computer.
● Get active for 20 minutes each day.

Junk food

Which foods are junk foods?

Junk foods have little goodness in them. They contain few vitamins. But they are high in fat, salt, and sugar. They include fries, burgers, chicken nuggets, fish sticks, many bottled sauces, chips, candy bars, cookies, and ice cream. Many precooked meals also contain too much fat, salt, or sugar.

How much junk food is okay?

Junk food is not good for your health. Try not to eat too much junk food, even if you like the taste of it. You will look nicer and be healthier without junk food.

Just awful!

- In the United States, more than half the people are overweight, and one in four are obese.
- Obesity is the second biggest killer in the United States after tobacco.
- Being overweight can cause diabetes, heart disease, strokes, cancer, and many other serious diseases.

eating...
Too little

many more children weigh too much than weigh too little. But some kids think it's cool to be as slim as a Barbie doll, Hollywood actor, or fashion model. Some think the thinner they are, the healthier they are. This is not true. The best way to stay healthy is to eat a balanced diet and take some exercise every day.

◄ *Eat healthy food, but don't skip any meals. You need to eat so your body grows and stays healthy.*

Food facts

Safety first!

● **If you think you are overweight...**
● Ask the school nurse to weigh you and to measure your BMI (body mass index). It will tell you if you really weigh too much for your age and height.

● Do not go on a diet. Only cut out certain foods if your doctor tells you to.
● If you are worried about your size and body image, discuss your feelings with your parents, the nurse, or your physician.

Eating problems....

Lack of appetite

When you are ill, you probably don't feel like eating a lot. This is normal. Don't worry about it—your appetite will soon come back. Try to eat several small meals during the day. Nibble on some dried fruit. Drink a fruity milk shake.

Food dislikes

If there are some foods you do not like at all, tell your parents. Try a different food from the same group. If you don't like potatoes, try rice or noodles, for example.

Eating pains

Eating should not be painful. If it hurts to eat, you must see the nurse or a physician. They will check if your throat, mouth, and stomach are healthy. They will help you get better quickly.

eat a variety of foods

eat healthy foods

Serious disorders!

Some people find it hard to eat anything. Some only eat in secret. This is called anorexia. Others eat a lot, then make themselves throw it all up. This is called bulimia. Anorexia and bulimia are dangerous eating disorders. Anyone with an eating disorder needs to get help from a parent, a nurse, a teacher, or a physician.

try out a new food

Food that can...
Make you sick

If food is not clean and safe, it can make you ill. Raw food and cooked leftovers need to be kept in the fridge. Cover them with foil and put them on different shelves. Keep the kitchen clean. Wipe up any spills. Take the garbage out often, especially on hot days. And clear away and wash dirty dishes after your meals.

◀ *Bad food can make you sick and give you a stomachache.*

Safety first!

- **Always be clean around food...**
- Wash your hands after going to the toilet, after stroking an animal, after touching garbage, and before eating.

- Don't eat any food, like bread or jam, that has gone moldy.
- Don't eat anything after its sell-by date.
- Keep pets out of the kitchen.

Food poisoning

Eating out and food to go

Sometimes food from a restaurant or snack bar is not very good. That could be because the kitchen is not clean or because the food itself is bad. If you feel ill after eating in a restaurant, tell your parents. They may need to take you to see a physician.

◀ *Germs can live in bowls of snack foods. Wash your hands before you eat.*

Eating too much junk food can also make you sick. Avoid too many doughnuts, sodas, fries, burgers...

What to do if...

● **...you feel sick after eating**
● Go to the bathroom to throw up.
● Afterward, lie down to relax.
● Do not eat until you feel better.

● Drink plenty of water, soda, or black tea with sugar. Start eating again slowly—try dry toast or chicken soup.
● If it happens often, see a physician.

How often and...
When to eat

nearly half of all children skip breakfast. Do you? After a long night without eating, it's important to have a good meal. It gives you an instant boost of all the foods you need to grow. Kids who eat breakfast do better at school. Is your family rushed in the morning? Does no one have time to sit around the breakfast table? Help with simple tasks to get ready.

◄ *A good, healthy breakfast sets you up for the whole day.*

Why is it good for me?

- **A good breakfast will...**
- Give you more energy to play.
- Help you grow strong and healthy.
- Stop you snacking on junk food later.

- Help you concentrate at school.
- Stop you having stomachaches.
- Help you get better grades at reading and math.

The eating day

Breakfast
The first and most important meal. Eat two servings from the grain group, one from the fruit group, and one from the milk group.

School lunch
Avoid fatty, deep-fried meat and fries. Choose fresh vegetables and fruit. Take your own packed lunch. Make it as exciting and interesting as you can.

Evening meal
Have a light meal in the evening. Eat early, then relax. Don't eat a huge meal just before you go to bed.

▲ *Put banana slices over your cereal for tasty flavor and extra vitamins.*

▶ *Try a soft-boiled egg. You can make toast "soldiers" and dip them into it.*

Or try this...

- Best breakfast ideas...
- waffles with strawberries or peach slices and yogurt
- apricot milk-smoothie

- honey on wholemeal toast
- toasted bagel with cheese
- mixed fruit kabobs with strawberry sauce dip

TIDAK HALAL

Food choices

not everyone eats everything. People have different reasons for refusing some foods. They may not like the taste of a particular food. Or they may have a disease like diabetes, which stops people eating sweets. Some religions have rules about what food people eat and when they should eat it. Vegetarians choose not to eat any meat.

◀ *Followers of Islam (a religion) are called Muslims. A Muslim family buys its meat from a halal butcher. Halal meat is butchered according to Muslim rules.*

Or try this...

- ● Some vegetarian treats...
- ● veggie burger made from soy beans
- ● spaghetti with pumpkin and nuts
- ● baked potato with pinto beans
- ● BBQ peppers, onions, and eggplant
- ● five-bean salad with eggs
- ● banana and mango juice
- ● grilled peaches with honey

▲ *Illness can also keep you from eating certain foods. Diabetics can only eat sweet food that has been specially made for them.*

Always check that your food does not contain anything that you are allergic to.

What are allergies?

Some people get very ill when they eat a food that they are allergic to. There are different sorts of **allergies** (AL ur jeez). Some people can't have milk or milk products, others can't eat nuts or gluten (gluten is a starch in bread, cookies, pasta, and cereals).

▶ *People with nut allergies get very ill if they eat nuts. Never give nuts to little children. They might choke on the nuts.*

Safety first!

!!!allergies can kill!!!

● Never give a person with an allergy a food to eat that he or she is allergic to.

● Always read labels carefully. Allergy-causing foods are not always obvious.
● If you or someone else has a strong allergic reaction go straight to a hospital.

Look forward to...
A healthy life

find the lifestyle that is right for you. Eat more if you are very active, less if you aren't. Choose healthy foods and drinks. Eat small amounts of less healthy foods. Cut out junk food altogether. Get more active, and you will have a healthy body, a lively mind, and feel happy.

▲ *Living a healthy life is not boring. It gives you energy to do what you want to do.*

Safety first!

● **Do eat and drink...**
- lots of water, fruit juice, and milk
- lots of colorful fruit and vegetables
- varied foods from different groups

Don't eat or drink...
- lots of sugary drinks
- food high in salt, sugar, or fat
- food mainly from one food group

Test yourself

Healthy food choices:

1. All these are fatty foods. Which one is healthiest?

A a large fruit-flavor ice cream
B a bag of mixed, unsalted nuts
C a cream cake with topping

2. To eat healthily you should...

A avoid all fat
B eat only small amounts of fat, choosing vegetable fats whenever possible
C slap on lots of cream

3. Which drink is healthy?

A a fresh fruit juice
B a small diet soda
C a large, sparkling fruit-flavor drink

Healthy lifestyle choices:

4. If you are overweight, you can lose weight by...

A making sensible food choices and getting active every day
B spending three hours every day exercising in the gym
C eating nothing for a week

5. If you don't like to eat meat, you should...

A try to eat it anyway
B eat lots of sweets instead
C eat a balanced diet with lots of vegetable proteins such as soy beans and legumes

ANSWERS: 1B, 2B, 3A, 4A, 5C

Food facts

eat lots of fruit and vegetables

eat wholemeal foods

avoid fats and sugars

Or try this...

● Think of fruits and vegetables starting with each letter of the alphabet—then try eating them over a few weeks.
● Try out a new fruit or veg each week.

● Learn how to grow vegetables. Then learn how to cook them.
● Compete with friends: Who can go without sweets the longest?

Glossary
What does it mean ?

allergies: *Allergic people become ill, get rashes, or breathing problems when they eat some foods or touch some things.*

calcium: *We need calcium for healthy teeth and bones. Milk and cheese contain lots of calcium.*

calories: *We measure food energy in calories. Many people eat more calories than they need.*

carbohydrates: *Starchy or sugary foods are full of carbohydrates. Carbohydrates give us energy.*

diabetes: *A diabetic cannot control the levels of sugar in her or his blood. Many diabetics are overweight, but not all.*

digest: *How your body breaks down the food that you eat.*

fiber: *An important part of our food. It makes the stomach work harder.*

heart disease: *A dangerous disease. The blood vessels are blocked or narrow. It is hard work for the heart to pump blood around the body, so the heart gets sick.*

obese: *very overweight. Ask your school nurse if you think you might be obese.*

organs: *Parts of our bodies, for example heart, lungs, stomach, kidneys, ears, or eyes. Each organ has a particular job.*

To find out more...

...check out these websites:
- www.americanheart.org
American Heart Association
- www.healthyfridge.org/justforkids.html
Open the fridge door to a healthy heart!
- www.healthykidschallenge.com
Activities, games, recipes, and challenges related to healthy eating.
- www.kidshealth.org
Loads of information on healthy eating.

overweight: *too fat. Ask your school nurse if you think you might be overweight.*

proteins: *We need to eat proteins for our bodies to grow and heal. Meat, fish, dairy foods, and legumes (vegetables such as beans and peas) are rich in proteins.*

starchy: *to contain a lot of starch. Pasta, potatoes, and rice are starchy foods.*

tissues: *Your body and its organs are made up of different tissues, such as skin.*

vegetarian: *A person who does not eat meat. Vegetarians called vegans also do not eat animal products, like butter or eggs.*

vitamins: *We need to eat tiny particles called vitamins to grow and stay healthy. Fruits and vegetables are rich in vitamins.*

To find out more...

...read these books

● Dawson, Susan, and Susan Norton, *Pyramid Pal—Adventures in Eating*. Griffin, 2000.
● Frost, Helen. *The Food Guide Pyramid*. Pebble Books, 2000.
● King, Hazel. *Carbohydrates for a Healthy Body*. Heinemann Library, 2003.
● Powell, Jillian. *Fats for a Healthy Body*. Heinemann Library, 2003.
● Royston, Angela. *Proteins for a Healthy Body*. Heinemann Library, 2003.
● Thomas, Ann. *Fats, Oils, and Sweets*. Chelsea House, 2002.

● www.nal.usda.gov/fnic
Food and Nutrition Information Center at the National Agricultural Library (NAL)
● www.nutritionexplorations.org/kids/main.asp

Games, activities, and fun recipes.
● www.obesity.org
American Obesity Association

Index
Which page is it on?